# The Haunted Apartment House Mystery

Elaine Pageler

**High Noon Books**
Novato, California

**Cover Design and Interior Illustrations: Tina Cash**



International Standard Book Number: 0-87879-986-9

3 2 1 0 9 8 7 6 5
0 9 8 7 6 5 4 3 2

## Contents

## CHAPTER 1

# The Star Is Haunted

Brad dropped his camera case on his desk. He had been taking pictures. It had been hot. Now he was tired and crabby.

He looked at Meg Green's desk. That girl had been a pest ever since the boss at the News said she and Brad were a team.

Meg didn't look at him. Instead she looked across the room. "I think you have a visitor," she said.

"Hello, Brad," called a voice.

An old man walked toward him. He used a cane.

Brad had seen that gray hair before. He knew those pale blue eyes, too. But who was this man? Where had he seen him?

The man held out a shaky hand. "I'm Cap Ambers. Your grandpa and I were friends," he said.

"Sure, you lived in the same apartment house. It was on Riddle Street. Wasn't it called the Star?" Brad asked.

Cap nodded. "I miss him," he said.

"I do, too," Brad said.

"At least he died before things got bad," Cap went on.

*The man held out a shaky hand.*

"What do you mean?" Brad asked.

A sad look came over Cap's face. "Things aren't good at the Star now. That's why I'm here. I need to move. But that takes money. Could you get me a job at the News?" he asked.

Brad didn't know what to say. Cap must be eighty-five. What could he do at the News?

"I'd be a good handy man," Cap said.

Brad paused. He wanted to help Cap.

Tears came to Cap's eyes. "You're my last chance. I've looked everywhere for work. No one wants an old man," he said.

"I'll try," Brad told him.

Brad left Cap at his desk. He went to see his boss.

Mr. Ross listened to Brad's story. "Cap's too old. We can't give him a job," he said.

Brad nodded. "I know. Could I say maybe we will have a job for him? That would give me time to find out what's wrong," Brad said.

Mr. Ross patted Brad on the back. "Sure, tell him to come back next week," he said.

Brad went back to his desk. Cap was not there. Instead he was sitting at Meg's desk. A cup was in his hand.

Meg looked up. "Cap and I had a talk. He told me about the Star. It's haunted. Did you know that?" she asked.

Brad couldn't believe his ears. "The Star is haunted?" he asked Cap.

"Yes, I didn't want to tell you. Your grandpa didn't believe stories about Zeke. So I didn't think you would," Cap said.

"Is Zeke the ghost?" Meg asked.

Cap nodded. "Most people have moved out. They're scared. What about your boss? Does he have a job for me?" he asked.

"I don't know. The boss says to come back next week. I'd like to talk some more. Will you be at the Star after lunch?" Brad asked.

Cap nodded. He turned to Meg. "Maybe I'll get a job here. Then I'll see you again," he said.

"Oh, you will see me right after lunch. I'm coming with Brad," she said.

# CHAPTER 2

## Brad Remembers

Brad headed for the Star. He could hear Meg's footsteps. She was tagging after him. Cap was his problem. Why did she have to come along?

"The Star was built in 1920. It has 5 floors and 25 apartments. One man owns it. He lives on the fifth floor," Meg called to him. She was trying to catch up to Brad.

Brad stopped. He turned and looked at her. "Where did you learn that?" he asked.

"It was easy. I used the phone," Meg said.

Brad was surprised. "Did you do that for Cap? You don't even know him," he said.

"No, but I know what people like to read. Here's our next Riddle Street Story," Meg said.

Brad turned and walked on. He was worried about Gramps' friend. But Meg only thought about the story. That was just like her.

Meg ran after him. "What do you know about the Star?" she asked.

"Gramps lived there. I would go to visit him. But the Star wasn't haunted," Brad said.

"A haunted apartment house sounded strange to me, too. So I called Mr. Carson. That's the owner. He'll talk to us today," Meg said.

"That's great. What time?" Brad asked.

"Mr. Carson said 3 o'clock," Meg said.

Brad looked at his watch. "That's an hour from now. We'll have time to talk to Cap."

The Star was on the corner. Once it had looked nice. Now it seemed old and shabby.

Brad pushed on the door. He and Meg went in.

The lobby was much the same. But now it seemed darker. Maybe it was because of the window. It was spotted with dirt.

A staircase was in the center. Brad looked up at it. He could see all 5 floors above.

An elevator was on one side. It had glass doors. They needed washing, too.

A TV sat in the back of the room. Cap and another man sat in front of it. They stared at the screen.

A woman was near them. She sat in a wheelchair. It was the kind with a motor. Four buttons were on the wheelchair's arm to make it move forward and backward.

Brad walked over to Cap. "Hi," he said.

Cap took Brad's hand. He turned to the other man. "Milt, do you remember Brad? He's Barker's grandson," he said.

"Sure, you came here a lot," Milt said.

Brad remembered Milt. He used to tell stories. They were about the Star's being haunted. But Gramps said they weren't true.

Cap turned to the woman in the wheelchair. "This is Mrs. Flood," he said.

Mrs. Flood wore glasses. She had white hair, too. It hung over most of her face.

Brad hadn't seen her before. "Are you new?" he asked.

"No, I've lived here for years," she said.

"You didn't meet her. Mrs. Flood was ill then. She couldn't get out of bed. Her niece Fay took care of her," Cap told him.

"Sure, I remember Fay. She fixed Gramps' watch once," Brad said.

"That's right. I remember that, too. Fay was handy with things like that. She fixed my TV, too," Cap said.

Mrs. Flood went on with her story. "I was very sick. At last I went to the hospital. They thought I was dying. But I got well. Fay got me this wheelchair. Now I can live alone," she told them.

"That's great. Where is Fay now?" Brad asked her.

"She went back to work," Mrs. Flood said.

"Is she a nurse?" Meg asked.

"No, she works for herself," Mrs. Flood told her.

"There must be others here I know. I met lots of Gramps' friends," Brad said.

Cap shook his head. "No, we're the only ones left. Everyone else moved out," he said.

"You forgot Chad Smith. He still lives here," Milt said.

"That's right. Chad is new. He moved here two years ago. There are just the four of us and the owner," Cap said.

"But there are 25 apartments in this building," Meg said.

"This place was full. What happened?" Brad asked.

"It's Zeke," Milt said.

The room got very quiet. The three old people looked across the room. Fear was on their faces.

## CHAPTER 3

# Zeke and the Elevator

The three old people didn't move. They still stared across the room. It seemed colder now. Brad felt a chill run up his back.

Meg broke the quiet. "Who is Zeke?" she asked.

Now Cap, Milt, and Mrs. Flood looked at Brad and Meg.

"Zeke is a ghost," Mrs. Flood said.

"Milt should tell you the story. He knows the most about Zeke," Cap said.

Brad turned to Milt. "How did you hear the story?" he asked.

Milt shook his head. "It's no story. I knew Zeke," he said.

"When was that?" Meg asked.

"It was about seventy years ago. Both of us lived here. I was twenty. This was my first apartment. It was on the first floor. Zeke was an old man. He lived on the fourth floor," Milt told them.

Brad looked up the staircase. "That's a long way up. It's good that the Star has an elevator," he said.

"The Star has one now. But it didn't then. That was the problem," Milt said.

"Did old Zeke climb all those stairs?" Brad asked.

Milt nodded. "Zeke wanted an elevator. He begged the owner to put one in. He asked many times. But Mr. Carson didn't," he said.

"Mr. Carson is the owner now. Is he the same man?" Meg asked.

"No, that was his father. One night Zeke tripped on the top stair. He fell all the way down. We all heard him. I lived on the first floor. So I was the first one to him. Zeke cursed the Star. He vowed to haunt it. Then he died," Milt told them.

"Milt told everyone what Zeke said. No one believed him until now," Cap added.

"Gramps lived here. Zeke didn't haunt the Star then," Brad said.

"Milt said he did. I never thought so. But things have changed. It started about two years ago," Cap said.

Mrs. Flood's eyes got big. "It happens at night. Zeke falls down the stairs. He moans and groans," she said.

"Zeke curses the Star. He says he'll haunt it always," Cap added.

"Does it happen every night?" Brad asked.

"Yes, it does," called a new voice.

A young man hung over the railing. Thick glasses were on his nose. "He does it again and again. None of us can sleep," he said.

"This is Chad. He's a writer," Cap said.

Chad came down the steps. "This is a bad place. I'm leaving when my book is done. I'd go now but I don't have the money," he said.

Brad looked at his watch. It was almost 3 o'clock. "We're going up to see Mr. Carson," he said.

He and Meg walked toward the elevator.

"Stop! Don't use that!" Cap said.

Mrs. Flood pushed a button. Her wheelchair moved toward them. "Zeke lives in there. He won't let any of us use it," she said.

Brad looked at Meg. This couldn't be true.

Meg smiled. Then she reached out to press the elevator button.

"Clang," went the elevator.

"Ha! Ha! Ha!" howled a deep voice. It came from the elevator.

Brad looked through the glass doors. No one was inside.

Up went the elevator. "This is my home," called the voice.

Meg's eyes were big. "I didn't touch the button," she said.

The laughing went on. Now it came from the fifth floor. "My home! My home!" called the deep voice.

Cold chills ran up Brad's back. Could these people be right? Did Zeke haunt the Star?

## CHAPTER 4

## Mr. Carson and the MML

Brad and Meg went up the stairs. Five flights were a lot. They huffed and puffed.

Mr. Carson met them at the top. The man looked about fifty.

He led them into his living room. "So you met Zeke," he said.

Brad nodded. "What's going on?" he asked.

"I wish I knew. But it won't be my problem after this week. I'm losing the Star. The MML is taking it away from me," Mr. Carson said.

"Who is the MML?" Meg asked.

Mr. Carson gave her their card. "The MML stands for Mock Money Lenders. I owe them a lot of money," he told them.

"Can't you sell the Star?" Brad asked.

"No one will buy it. They've heard of Zeke," Mr. Carson said.

Meg kept looking at the card. "I've never heard of the MML," she said.

"Nor had I. But then Zeke came. People started moving out. I had to have money. MML sent me letters. They gave me a better deal than banks. I took money from them. Things got worse. I took more money. Now they're taking the Star," Mr. Carson told them.

"Did you tell the police about Zeke?" Brad asked.

Mr. Carson nodded. "I talked to Sergeant Ward. They don't check out ghosts," he said.

"I've got an idea. Give me a room for a few days. I'll check out Zeke," Brad said.

Mr. Carson's face lit up. He handed Brad a key. "You can have 304. A man just moved out. It still has everything in it," he said.

Brad and Meg left. They walked down the stairs.

"We better talk to the MML. They're on High Street," Meg said.

Once again, Meg had a good idea. Brad had to admit it. "All right let's go," he said.

The three old people were still in the lobby. They watched Brad and Meg come down the stairs.

"Thanks for coming by," Cap said.

Brad showed them his key. "I'm moving in," he told them.

A shocked look came to everyone's face. They stared at Brad.

"There's a ghost," Mrs. Flood said.

"I'm not afraid of Zeke," Brad told her.

"What room do you have?" Milt asked.

"It's 304," Brad said.

There was a sound above. Brad looked up. Chad was leaning over the rail. But he didn't say anything.

Brad and Meg hurried down Riddle Street. They turned on High. The MML was in a big building. But it had just two small rooms. The first had a desk and a file case. The door to the second room was closed. It must lead to the boss.

A girl sat at the desk. A large stack of books were near her. She was reading one of them. These were mystery books. The girl must not have much to do.

The girl looked up. "May I help you?" she asked.

"I would like a loan," Brad said.

"Sorry, we aren't giving loans," the girl told him.

"Could I speak to your boss?" Brad asked.

"The boss is out of town," the girl said.

Meg leaned forward. She bumped the books. They fell to the floor.

Brad glared at her. Meg was a pest. Did she have to be clumsy, too?

The girl had started to pick up the books. Brad dropped to the floor. He helped her. At last, all the books were picked up.

Brad led the way down the hall. "Watch what you're doing next time," he told Meg.

Meg smiled. "Why? That gave me time. I looked in the file case. Guess what? There's just one file in there. Mr. Carson is their only loan," she said.

## CHAPTER 5

# The Fire Escape

Brad stopped on Riddle Street. "I'm going home and get some clothes. Then I'm going back to the Star. I'll see you tomorrow," he said.

Meg smiled and walked away.

Brad got back to the Star within an hour. A bag of clothes was in his hand.

An old man sat outside the door. It was Cap. "I'm getting some sun," he said.

Brad went inside. No one was in the lobby. He walked to the third floor.

His room was locked. Brad reached for his key. That's when he heard it. There was a sound. It came from inside his room. Was it Meg?

Brad opened the door. No one was there. Wait! The back window was open. The wind blew the shades. Brad ran back to it. He looked out.

A fire escape went past the window. A man was running down it. He wore wore dark clothes and a hood over his face.

Was this a man or a woman? Brad wasn't sure. Could this be a robber? There wasn't much in the room to take. Maybe this was about Zeke and the Star.

Brad climbed out the window. He raced after the man. They went down the fire escape.

*He climbed back in a window.*

The man was almost to the ground. Brad thought he would run down the street. But the man didn't. He climbed back in a window.

Brad raced to the window. He climbed in. This was the basement. It was dark. He heard footsteps going away.

At last, Brad found a light. He turned it on. The man was gone.

There were stairs. They led up to the lobby. Brad dashed up, No one was in the lobby.

Just then the door opened. Cap came in. "The sun's getting low," he said.

"Did a guy come out of this door?" Brad asked.

"No one came out," Cap said.

The man hadn't gone outside. That meant he was still in the Star. Did he live here?

"But someone went in about five minutes ago. It was Meg," Cap went on.

"Oh, no, not Meg again," Brad thought.

What was she doing here? That girl never let him alone. Still, Brad would be glad to see her. He could tell her what happened.

Meg was waiting for him on the third floor. She was in front of his door.

"What are you doing here?" Brad asked.

"I brought dinner. It's inside. Where have you been?" Meg asked.

Brad headed for the door. "I'll tell you while we eat," he said.

Meg grabbed his arm. "Tell me out here," she said.

Brad frowned. The food sounded good. Why did Meg want to stay out in the hall?

"Well, where were you?" Meg asked.

Brad told her about the man. "I don't know why he was in my room," he said.

"I do. Be quiet and follow me," she said.

Meg went into his room. She pointed to the plant on the table.

Brad walked over to it. Something was under one leaf. He knew what it was. Someone had bugged his room. It must have been the man. He wanted to hear what Brad was saying.

## CHAPTER 6

# Sounds in the Night

Brad and Meg ate dinner at the table. The plant sat in the center. Someone was listening. They talked about shows and sports. But they didn't talk about Zeke or the Star.

Then they went out to the hall. There they could talk. No one could hear them if they spoke low.

Brad moved close to Meg. "That guy must work with the MML. They're trying to steal the Star," he said.

"Yes, they made everyone think there was a ghost. That made them move out," Meg said.

There was a sound. It came from the floor below.

"Look at that. Chad is coming out of his room," Meg said.

Brad watched him. Chad was short and thin. He could have been the man on the fire escape.

Chad walked back and forth. Then he went back in.

"He was the one in my room," Brad said.

Meg shook her head. "He wouldn't have had time. I saw him in a store two blocks away. That's when I came here," she said.

"Are you sure?" Brad asked.

"I wasn't close. But it looked like him," Meg said.

"You must be wrong. It had to be Chad. The guy moved fast. No one else could do that. Cap, Milt and Mrs. Flood are old. That leaves Mr. Carson. I don't think it was him," Brad said.

"Nor do I. It's late. I should go. Have a good time with Zeke. I'll be back tomorrow," Meg said.

"I'll walk you to the door," Brad said.

The three old people were in the lobby. Cap and Milt watched TV. Mrs. Flood had her eyes closed. A radio was in her lap. Earphones were on her ears. Her feet tapped. She must be hearing music.

Cap saw Brad and Meg. He turned off the TV.

"Mrs. Flood, turn off your radio. Brad and Meg are here," Cap shouted at her.

Mrs. Flood shut it off. She pulled off her earphones, too. "I like music at night. It helps my nerves," she said.

"Zeke will start soon. We all stay here until he's done. It's safer that way," Cap said.

"Does Chad come down, too?" Brad asked.

"No, he stays in his room. Here's some chairs. Come and join us," Milt said.

"No, I'm going home," Meg said.

"And I'm going up to my room. It's been a

long day," Brad told them.

Brad climbed the stairs. He went in his room and sat down. Time went by. Brad's eyes started to close.

"Crash! Bump, bump, bump!" came a loud noise.

It sounded like someone was falling down the stairs. Then a voice started to moan. "I'll haunt the Star always!" it yelled.

Brad raced out to the hall. He looked over the railing. No one was there. Brad could feel his heart pounding.

Then it started again. Brad heard Zeke fall down the stairs. The sounds came from all over. But they were loudest just above his head. That was strange. Zeke had fallen to the lobby.

Brad looked up. There was a heating vent. It was in the ceiling above him.

An idea popped into Brad's head. He rushed up to the fourth floor. The noise started. Again it was loudest by the heating vent.

Brad went to the other floors, too. But he didn't go to the lobby. The same thing was true. The sounds were loudest by the vents.

"A speaker is in each vent," he thought.

There were tools in his bag. Brad got them and pulled out a chair. Then he went to work. Soon the vent was open. There sat the speaker.

It was as Brad had thought. Zeke was just sounds on a tape. But who was playing it?

## CHAPTER 7

# The Remote Control

Everyone was still asleep the next day. Brad took his tools. He went to the elevator in the lobby. Nothing happened. It didn't move and Zeke didn't laugh. Brad thought he knew why.

He stepped inside and took off the control board. There was a speaker in back of it. That's where Zeke's laugh came from.

Then he saw something else. Wires went to a box. Brad knew what it was. It was for a remote control.

Someone could stand across the room. He could push a button. It would make the elevator go up or down.

Brad put the board back. Then he went to his room.

Where was Meg? For once he wanted to see her. She needed to know about this.

Time went by. At last Meg tapped on his door. Her notebook was in her hand.

Brad stepped out in the hall. He told her about the elevator and the remote control.

"I've got news, too. Guess who owns the MML? It's Fay Mock," Meg said.

"That's Mrs. Flood's niece. She stayed here when the old woman was ill," Brad said.

"There's something else, too," Meg said. She gave Brad her notebook.

Brad read the page. "That's it. Now we know who it is. You phone Sergeant Ward. I'll get everyone to the lobby," he said.

It was an hour later. Everyone was in the lobby. Cap, Milt and Mr. Carson sat on chairs. Mrs. Flood was in her wheelchair. Chad stood by the stairs.

Sergeant Ward stayed near the door. "I don't deal with ghosts," he said.

"There's no ghost. It's a thief. Someone's trying to steal the Star," Brad told him.

"Zeke's a ghost. Everyone's heard him," Milt said.

Brad shook his head. "Everyone heard your story. One of them made a plan. It was to make all of you think Zeke was here," he said.

Cap looked at Brad. "But Zeke does haunt the Star. We hear him," he said.

"Have you ever seen him?" Meg asked.

"No one sees a ghost," Milt said.

"Zeke isn't a ghost. It's a tape. Speakers are in all of the heating vents," Brad told them.

"It all started two years ago," Meg said.

"Lots of things happened. Mrs. Flood came back and Chad moved in. Zeke started haunting the Star. People moved out. The MML wrote Mr. Carson letters. They loaned him money," Brad went on.

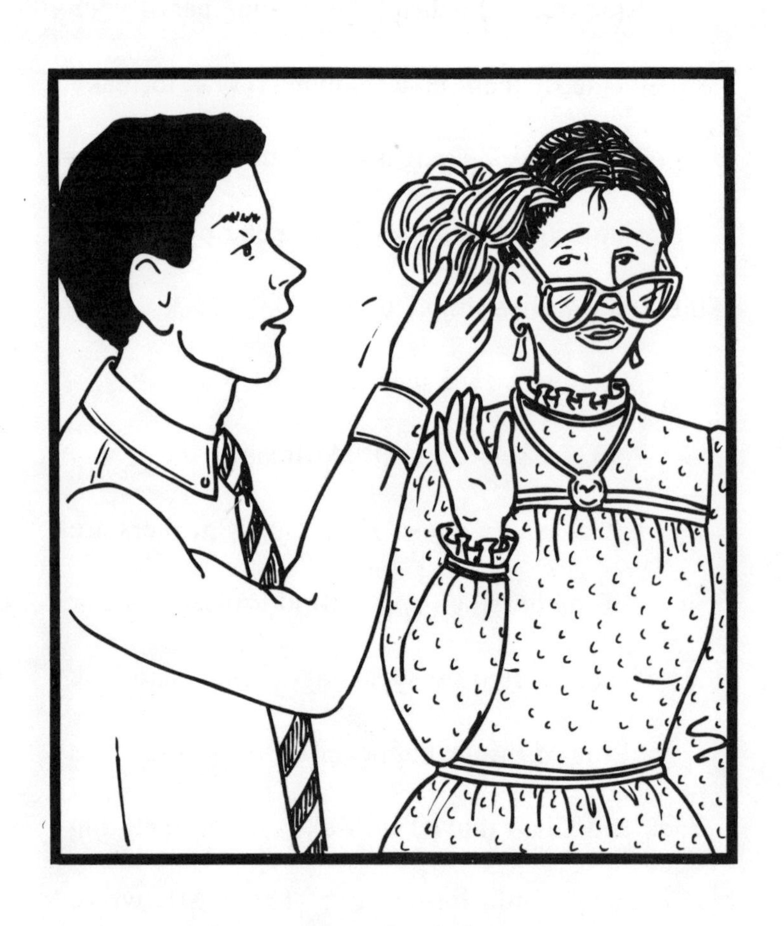

*He gave Mrs. Flood's hair a tug.*

Mr. Carson's eyes lit up. "Zeke scared people away. The MML loaned me money. They worked with each other," he said.

"No, it's the same person," Brad told him.

Chad backed away. "I know what you're thinking. But it isn't me," he said.

"No, it isn't. The owner of the MML is Fay Mock," Brad told them.

Cap looked up at Brad. "That's Mrs. Flood's niece. Where is she?" he asked.

"Right here," said Brad.

He gave Mrs. Flood's hair a tug. It came off. So did her glasses. There sat a much younger woman.

"Fay!" everyone gasped.

Brad pushed the buttons of her wheelchair. One made the elevator go. Another made the sound of Zeke's fall down the stairs.

"Mrs. Flood lives in a rest home. Fay came here. She put in the speakers and the remote control at night. You know she's good at fixing things," Brad said.

Sergeant Ward looked at Brad and Meg. "You're good at fixing things, too," he said.

"Go up and get your camera. We have a story to do," Meg told Brad.

That was just like Meg. But Brad didn't mind. She didn't seem like a pest today.

Brad grinned at her. "I'll be right back," he said.